Little, Brown and Company
Hachette Book Group
1290 Avenue of the Americas, New York, NY 10104
Visit us at lb-kids.com
mylittlepony.com

First Edition: August 2017

Little, Brown and Company is a division of Hachette Book Group, Inc.
The Little, Brown name and logo are trademarks of Hachette Book Group, Inc.

The publisher is not responsible for websites (or their content) that are not owned by the publisher.

Library of Congress Control Number: 2017942703

ISBNs: 978-0-316-55770-2 (hardcover), 978-0-316-55775-7 (ebook), 978-0-316-55774-0 (ebook),
978-0-316-55771-9 (ebook)

Printed in the United States of America

PHX

10 9 8 7 6 5 4 3 2 1

Licensed By:

The Great Princess Caper

By Michael Vogel

Illustrated by Amy Mebberson

Little, Brown and Company
New York Boston

Once upon a time in a faraway land—
a land very different from Equestria—there lived an evil ruler.

The Storm King was a bully who used his army
of **powerful, mean,** and **scary** soldiers to force
everycreature to do whatever he wanted!

But there was one member of the Storm Guards who was different from the rest. He wasn't **powerful.** He wasn't **mean.** And as hard as he tried, he wasn't very **scary.** His name was Grubber.

Grubber wanted to fit in, though, so he practiced every day.

He practiced being **powerful,** but he wasn't that strong.
He practiced being **mean,** but everycreature laughed at him.
He practiced being **scary,** but he just looked silly.

For the most part, nocreature paid any attention at all to Grubber.

Everycreature knows that nocreature pays any attention to you when you're small!

At least, that's what Grubber thought until the day a stranger appeared....

She was something called a *pony*—a Unicorn, to be exact—and she had a horn that was broken and crackly. Her name was Tempest Shadow, and she was small… almost as small as Grubber, and *much* smaller than the Storm Guards.

She should have been ignored by everycreature.
But she wasn't.

She was **powerful.**

She was **mean.**

She was **scary.**

Everycreature paid attention to Tempest!

Grubber wanted to be

JUST.
LIKE.
HER.

Tempest made a deal with the Storm King. She would help him become the most **powerful** ruler in all the land if he promised to restore her broken horn.

The Storm King agreed and gave Tempest control of his Storm Guards. With Tempest leading his army, the Storm King grew **more and more powerful.**

Grubber followed Tempest everywhere she went.

"Let me be your loyal sidekick!" he begged.

"I don't need one," Tempest sneered in reply.

Grubber tried to stow away on her ship, but she kicked him off.

He tried to disguise himself, but she knew it was him. He even tried begging, but she refused him **again and again.**

Finally, Tempest had had enough.

"*Fine!*" she growled. "You can come on my next mission and try to prove yourself. If you *do*, you can be my sidekick. If you *don't*, you leave me alone forever."

"*Deal!*" Grubber said, shaking Tempest's hoof. "By the time we're done, you'll wonder how you ever managed without me! What's the mission?"

"We're invading *Equestria*," Tempest revealed. "A land filled with weak, defenseless ponies. We're going to steal their magic and give it to the Storm King. Then he will restore my horn."

"Ponies? Is it your home? Are we going to see your family and friends?" Grubber asked. (He loved a good family vacation.)

"It's not my home anymore. And I have no friends," Tempest said. "Now prepare my ship."

Grubber was excited. This was his first official invasion. He spent the journey working on his arrival speech to the ponies. He wanted to make sure it sounded **powerful, mean,** and **scary!**

When the ship arrived in Canterlot, Grubber walked down the gangway and cleared his throat.

"Ponies of Equestria!" he said in his most intimidating voice. "We come on behalf of the fearsome, the powerful, the almighty...*Storm King*!"

He expected ponies to be shaking in their horseshoes. But they just looked confused.

Disappointed, he finished the speech: "And now to deliver his evil, evil message...put your hooves together for *Commander Tempest Shadow*!"

Tempest appeared. Everypony in the crowd shook with fear at the sight of her. She explained to the princesses that she was going to take their magic the easy way or the hard way.

The princesses chose the hard way…which was just what Tempest wanted!

She was **powerful.**

She was **mean.**

She was **scary.**

One by one, she turned the princesses to stone!
Well, almost all the princesses. One princess, the
smallest, managed to escape with her friends.
Tempest was furious. She ordered Grubber to
bring the final princess to her.

This was Grubber's chance to prove he was
a good sidekick!

Grubber and a battalion of Storm Guards **chased** the princess and her friends through the city. But the ponies **escaped** over the edge of a giant waterfall! Grubber knew he was supposed to catch her. But he couldn't swim.

The princess got away.

SPLASH!

When Grubber explained what had happened, Tempest was *mad*. She needed all four princesses!

"I know you're disappointed. I got two words for you." Grubber revealed a piece of cake he had saved just for her.

Sponge cake!

But Tempest didn't want sponge cake— she wanted the runaway princess! Grubber was going to have to work *extra* hard to prove himself now.

poof

Tempest ordered Grubber to prepare her ship. They tracked the princess and her friends far to the south of Equestria, past the Badlands, to a strange city built on the side of a cliff. Grubber tried to be helpful, but Tempest was used to doing everything herself.

She was **powerful.**

She was **mean.**

She was **scary.**

And she eventually discovered that the princess and her friends had stowed away on a ship! Tempest was close to getting her hooves on the princess, but Grubber was still no closer to proving himself!

Grubber steered their ship through the sky as they searched for the ponies. He was trying to figure out what he could do to convince Tempest he was a good sidekick when a giant rainbow **exploded** in the sky!

"Look at that rainbow!" Grubber exclaimed. "Whoa! That's so cool!"

"Yeah," Tempest said calmly. "Cool of them to let us know where they are."

Grubber smacked his forehead as Tempest took control of her ship. Of *course* the ponies made the rainbow! Another chance to prove himself ruined.

SMACK!

Tempest and Grubber boarded the other ship. But the captain and her crew insisted there were no ponies anywhere. Tempest was sure the princess and her friends were on board. She was sure she knew where they were.

But when she looked, it seemed as if the princess had **escaped** once again!

Grubber searched the ship for clues. If he found something that would help Tempest capture the princess, he could prove himself to Tempest for sure!

Unfortunately, he didn't find much. Just some doodles on a piece of paper and a cupcake.

He thought Tempest might be hungry and want the cupcake. But she was more interested in the doodles. They were drawn on a map! And it showed *exactly* where the princess was going!

Mount Aris!

Tempest took control of their ship. She flew them to Mount Aris and, sure enough, she found what she was after. And it was even better than she expected! The princess was alone, without any friends to help her.

Tempest made her move. The princess was **hers!**

Tempest made it back to Equestria just in time for the Storm King's arrival.

Now that the Storm King was there, Tempest didn't pay any attention to Grubber.

She ignored him, just like everycreature else did.

No matter what Grubber tried, it seemed like he was never good enough. He saw some cake on a wagon nearby. He figured maybe that would make him feel better.

He grabbed a handful of icing and saw two eyes staring back at him. It was the princess's friends!

This was Grubber's **last chance** to prove himself!

"Guards!" Grubber cried.

If he could stop the princess's friends, Tempest would *surely* want him to be her sidekick. He ordered the Storm Guards to attack. A great battle broke out! Grubber tried his hardest to be valuable.

He tried to be **powerful.** He tried to be **mean.** He tried to be **scary.**

As the battle raged, a storm ripped through the sky. Ponies and Storm Guards flew everywhere. Grubber realized he wasn't **powerful** enough, **mean** enough, *or* **scary** enough.

Grubber was small and scared. And so he hid.

When the storm finally ended, Grubber peeked out of his hiding spot. The battle was over and Equestria had been magically restored! Everything looked exactly like it had before the attack. The **powerful, mean,** and **scary** Storm Guards were running away! It looked as if the ponies had won!

Grubber was alone. Nopony was paying any attention to him. Just like usual.

Grubber didn't see Tempest anywhere. But it didn't really matter. He had failed. There was no way she would ever want him as a sidekick.

WHOO-HOO!

Hurrraaay!

Yeah!

As ponies cheered and celebrated, Grubber gathered some cupcakes and got ready to leave.

Just as he was about to go, he heard somepony calling his name.

"Grubber!" Tempest saw him and came rushing over. "There you are! I have to tell you something!"

"I know. I'm a terrible sidekick. I'll leave you alone forever. Good-bye."

"What? No! I wanted to give you this." Tempest gave Grubber a cupcake with the word **Sidekick** hastily written in icing on top!

"What is this?" he asked. "I'm not your sidekick! I didn't help you at *all*."

"That's because what I was doing was pretty evil," Tempest explained. "And you aren't very good at being an evil sidekick."

Grubber was confused. But Tempest laughed!

"You aren't powerful. You aren't mean, and you're certainly not scary. But you *are* generous. And you *are* loyal. And you make everypony laugh. And for my next mission, that's going to be very important!"

"So you *do* want me to be your sidekick?" Grubber asked.

"I want you to be my friend!" Tempest said, smiling.

"So what's our mission?" Grubber asked.

"Well," Tempest said, "the Storm King has been defeated by a princess using the most powerful magic of all: *friendship*. Somepony has to spread the word!"

And so Tempest, along with her amazing sidekick *and* good friend, Grubber, left Equestria to tell others about friendship. Together, they had many amazing adventures and accomplished many amazing things. But most important, they were the most amazing of friends.

And of course…

...they lived happily ever after.

The End